The Cellist of Sarajevo

STEVEN GALLOWAY

Level 3

Retold by Annette Keen
Series Editors: Andy Hopkins and Jocelyn Potter

Pearson Education Limited
Edinburgh Gate, Harlow,
Essex CM20 2JE, England
and Associated Companies throughout the world.

ISBN: 978-1-4082-9137-5

This edition first published by Pearson Education Ltd 2013

1 3 5 7 9 10 8 6 4 2

Text copyright © Pearson Education Ltd 2013
Illustrations by Jonathan Burton

Set in 11/14pt Bembo
Printed in China
SWTC/01

Published by Pearson Education Limited in association with
Penguin Books Ltd, and both companies being subsidiaries of Pearson PLC

For a complete list of the titles available in the Penguin Readers series please go to
www.penguinreaders.com. Alternatively, write to your local Pearson Education office
or to: Penguin Readers Marketing Department, Pearson Education,
Edinburgh Gate, Harlow, Essex CM20 2JE, England.

Contents

Introduction

It's been over a month since the family had electricity for more than a few hours. It's been even longer since they had running water. Life is difficult without electricity, but it's impossible without water.

The siege of Sarajevo – the capital of Bosnia and Herzegovina – began in April 1992 and ended almost four years later. In that time, about 10,000 people were killed in the city and 56,000 people were seriously hurt. Ten thousand flats and many other buildings in the city were destroyed.

In May 1992, twenty-two people were killed in Sarajevo while they waited in a line for bread. Every day for the next twenty-two days Vedran Smajlović, a local cellist, played Albinoni's Adagio in G Minor in that same street. Steven Galloway, a Canadian writer, heard Smajlović's story and wrote *The Cellist of Sarajevo*, but Galloway's book is a work of fiction. The real cellist's story was only the starting point for his book.

The Cellist of Sarajevo tells the stories of four people living in Sarajevo. Life is difficult and dangerous. There isn't enough food, water or medicine. People are killed crossing the road. Nobody can leave the city. The people of Sarajevo have to change their way of life. It is a very different life from life before the war.

The Cellist of Sarajevo is Steven Galloway's third book, and it is an international bestseller. Galloway teaches at the University of British Columbia, in Canada. He lives near Vancouver, with his wife and two daughters.

In the ruins of the Dresden Music Library, an Italian musician found a very small part of a piece of music.

Chapter 1 A City Under Siege

Sarajevo, 1992. There are snipers in the hills around the city and danger is everywhere. There is no electricity most days, and very little food. People have to carry water across town to their homes. Slowly, the men in the hills are destroying Sarajevo.

Dresden, in 1945, was another city destroyed by war. In the ruins of the Dresden Music Library, an Italian musician found a very small part of a piece of music. He believed that this was the work, from the 1800s, of Tomaso Albinoni, a Venetian. The musician took the little piece of music and worked on it for twelve years. The final work is known as Albinoni's Adagio. Most people think it is quite different to Albinoni's other work. But everyone agrees that it is very beautiful.

Nearly fifty years later, Albinoni's Adagio is the favourite piece of music of a cellist in Sarajevo. He likes the idea that it was rebuilt from almost nothing. He likes to think that something beautiful came from a terrible war. It gives him hope for the future. In Sarajevo, in 1992, hope is all that most people have.

And so, today, like every other day, the cellist sits at the window of his flat, playing his cello. He plays until his hope returns. Before the war, he was a well-known musician in Sarajevo and music made his life complete. On stage, in his tuxedo, he knew who he was. Now, there's nowhere to play. His tuxedo hangs in the cupboard in a plastic bag. It's been there since the war took everything from him. His parents are dead, his family home is destroyed, his life as a professional musician is finished. But he still plays for himself. Most days, he can play anything and the music brings him hope. On very bad days, he needs the Adagio. He knows that it won't help

1

him forever. There are not many Adagios left in him. He saves the piece for times when he really needs it.

The cellist looks down from his window. Outside, in the street, a line of people wait to buy bread. There hasn't been any bread in the market for more than a week and many of his friends and neighbours are in the line. The cellist thinks about joining them. But, in the end, he decides not to go.

Suddenly, a loud scream shoots down from the sky. Then the world outside his window explodes.

For a long time the cellist stands in his flat, looking down onto the street. He sees a woman's bag, covered with blood. There are many dead bodies, and people crying out for help. He looks down at the floor. He sees that he's dropped his bow. He can't explain why, but he walks to his cupboard and takes out his tuxedo.

He stands at his window all night and all through the next day. Then, at four o'clock in the afternoon, he picks up his bow. It's exactly twenty-four hours since his friends and neighbours died in the bread line. He carries his cello and a chair down the stairs to the empty street. The explosion has left a large hole in the ground. The cellist puts his chair down there and sits quietly. Then he lifts his bow and starts to play the Adagio. He tells himself that he will do this every day for twenty-two days. A day for each person who was killed. Or he'll try. He doesn't know if he will live through the next twenty-two days.

◆

Arrow is waiting. She can see three soldiers on the hill above Sarajevo. They probably think they're too far away for a sniper's bullet. They're wrong. Perhaps they think that nobody can get a bullet through the buildings between them and her. Again, they're wrong. She can kill any one of them, and maybe even two of them. She can do it any time she chooses. And soon she'll make her decision.

The soldiers have good reason to feel comfortable. They're almost a kilometre away from Arrow. Her rifle is the same kind as all the defenders use. Usually, it can kill a man eight hundred metres away. More than that, and a bullet probably won't reach. But Arrow is different. She can send a bullet to places that others can't. She can't understand why it's so difficult for them.

Arrow is hiding in an empty office building near the city centre. She's lying on her stomach on the floor, a few metres back from the ninth floor window. She has a good view of the hills to the south of Sarajevo, to the place where the three soldiers are standing. She can see them, but they can't see her.

Arrow believes that she's different from the snipers on the hills. She shoots only soldiers. They shoot ordinary men, women and children crossing the street. Every time they kill a person, they're trying to kill the city. Little by little, they're destroying the Sarajevo that Arrow remembers.

Arrow is twenty-eight and her real name is not Arrow. She remembers a beautiful city with lovely old buildings and parks. Sarajevo was famous for its theatre, music and art. It was a place where people lived together happily. When the fighting started, she changed her name to Arrow. To kill soldiers, she needed a different name. She became a person who hated. One day, she hopes, she can stop hating and killing. Then she can use her real name again.

When Arrow shoots one of the three soldiers, she'll be in danger immediately. Every sniper on the hills to the south will start to look for her. They will shell the building. But by then she'll be gone.

One of the three soldiers moves away from the other two. Then he moves out of the line of her bullet and saves his life.

One of the other soldiers laughs, then they both turn their heads. Arrow chooses one man and shoots. Her bullet finds the soldier and he falls to the ground. She gets ready to shoot again. But something is wrong. She realises that the men on the hill were looking for her all the time. They were waiting. Now they know exactly where she is. She moves quickly to her right. A bullet hits the floor at the place where she lay just a short time before.

She runs to the stairs. A shell hits the building and the explosion almost knocks Arrow off her feet. When she reaches the seventh floor, another shell hits. Large pieces of metal and wood start to crash onto the stairs. Arrow jumps down to the next floor and runs faster. She hears another shell as she reaches the ground floor. She leaves the office building by the back door, so the men on the hill don't see her. Then she runs. When she gets to the end of the street, she slows down. There is a pain in her side, but it's only a small cut. As Arrow walks towards the city centre, it starts to rain.

♦

Another day has just begun. Kenan is in the kitchen. His wife, Amila, and their three children are still asleep in the sitting-room at the back of the flat. The street-facing bedrooms are in a more dangerous position, so they don't use them now.

Kenan reaches for the plastic container that holds the family's final quarter-litre of water. He's forty years old, but he feels like an old man. He moves slowly and he's become thin.

It's been over a month since the family had electricity for more than a few hours. It's been even longer since they had running water. Life is difficult without electricity, but it's impossible without water. So every four days, Kenan takes his plastic containers and he walks across town to the brewery. It's one of the only places in the city to get clean drinking water. It's a journey with many crossroads on the way, and because of the snipers there's danger at all of them.

Kenan sits at the kitchen table and looks carefully at his six water containers. He checks for small holes. He makes sure that each container has the correct top. How much water should a person carry? It's a difficult decision. Too little, and you have to go back more often. Nobody wants to do this because of the danger from snipers. Too much, and it's difficult to run. The six containers will hold about twenty-four litres of water.

He finishes checking his containers and hears his wife coming through from the sitting-room.

'It was quiet last night,' he says. 'It won't be too bad out there today.'

But they both know that a quiet night doesn't mean a quiet day.

The children are awake now. Kenan kisses Amila. He wants to leave before they get out of bed. The door to the flat closes quietly behind him. He sits down on the top step and puts his head in his hands. He doesn't want to go. His legs are heavy and his hands are cold. He wants to go back to bed. He wants to sleep until the war ends. He wants his family to have their lives back again.

Kenan hears the children's voices in the flat and pushes himself to his feet. He doesn't want them to see him like this. He doesn't want them to know how afraid he is. If he doesn't return today, he doesn't want his fear to be their last memory of their father.

He picks up his water containers. He's tied them all together with a rope through the handles. They're light and easy to carry now. It will be more difficult when they're full of water and heavier. Kenan knows he's getting weaker, like everyone in the city. What will happen when he can't carry enough water for his family? Will he have to take his young son with him? He hopes not.

♦

Some days, it seems that there have always been men with guns on the hills. But Dragan still remembers how the city was before the war. Sarajevo was a great city for walking. You couldn't get lost – you just went downhill to the river and then you knew the way. People were happy in the city. Life was good. This is how Dragan remembers it. He knows that you can't walk from one end of the city to the other now. The men in the hills control areas like Grbavica and nobody goes near them. The post office, government buildings and library are all burned to the ground. The trains don't run. The streets are full of old cars and lorries, burned and useless. Every time you go outside, you're in danger. The same is true if you stay inside.

Dragan has been on the streets for about an hour today. He's trying to get from his home in the middle of town to the city's bakery. He's worked at the bakery for almost forty years. He's lucky to have this job. Most people in the city have no work at all. He doesn't get paid in money, but he's given bread. Also, he can eat in the workers' café free every day, even on days when he isn't working. Today, he's going there to eat.

Before the war, Dragan lived in a nice flat just west of Grbavica. Now, the building is almost destroyed and it's on the front line of the fighting. He knows he will never go back there. He lives north of the old town now, in his sister's flat, with her family.

Dragan's wife, Raza, and their eighteen-year-old son left the city before the fighting started. He thinks they're now in Italy. He doesn't know when he'll hear from them again. Dragan is sixty-four and Raza is six years younger. They had a comfortable life together. He hopes that she and their son are happy now. He's glad that they don't have to live with his sister's family. Dragan and his brother-in-law don't enjoy spending time together, but the family needs Dragan's bread and he needs a home.

It's only about three kilometres from his sister's flat to the bakery. Before the war, it was a forty-five minute walk. These days, it takes about an hour and a half if he hurries. Today he doesn't have to hurry and he's walked slowly most of the way. But at the place where the main road meets the Vrbanja Bridge, Dragan ran. He tried not to think about snipers.

Now he's on the road that they call 'Sniper Street'. It's the road that takes the foreign reporters from the airport to the Holiday Inn hotel. It probably seems very dangerous to them. The people of Sarajevo know that there are worse places than this.

Dragan leaves Sniper Street and soon reaches another crossing. Across the street is one of the city's largest office buildings. Shells have hit it so many times that it's now almost completely destroyed.

There are about twenty people waiting at the crossing. Dragan stands behind a wall. He's waiting until he can cross safely. He's seen three people killed at crossings. He's always surprised at how quickly it happens. One minute they're running, then suddenly there's the sound of a gunshot and the person falls. After a few minutes, everything is as it was before. The dead are taken away. Nobody knows if the sniper is still there. But slowly people start crossing again.

As Dragan waits at the crossroads, a man starts to cross from the other side. He runs with his head down, a cigarette in his mouth. Dragan remembers him. His name is Amil. He sold newspapers near Dragan's old flat.

Amil reaches the other side. As he gets close, Dragan turns away from him. They often talked together before the war, but that was then. Dragan doesn't talk to any of his friends these days, and visits nobody. At work, he says as little as possible. He has lost so much in this war. People have died or changed; everyone has become a stranger.

In front of him, two people decide to cross – a man and a woman in their thirties, he thinks. They step into the street. They start to move quickly, not quite running. They're almost in the middle when a bullet hits the road in front of the man. They stop. Then the man pulls the woman to him and they run together towards the other side of the street. There's the sound of another shot, but either they're lucky or the sniper makes a mistake. They reach the other side. For a few minutes, none of the other people try to cross.

Dragan doesn't feel ready to go. He waits.

Chapter 2   A Special Job

Kenan walks downhill towards the old town. He started every day like this before the war. Kenan worked in an office, but the building is now destroyed. If he tries really hard, he can forget the siege. He can imagine he's going to work. Perhaps he'll have lunch with his friend Goran. Maybe they'll sit in Veliki Park with a coffee.

But soon he arrives at a crossing where there's a pile of shelled cars. Now he can't forget that his city is at war. He remembers the water containers again and he hears gunfire in the city. He also remembers that Veliki Park is one of the most dangerous parts of Sarajevo. He hasn't seen Goran for months. Kenan thinks he's dead.

He looks up at the hills. He can't see the soldiers there, but they can probably see him. If they can, they'll see nothing unusual about Kenan. He's a thin man in an old brown coat,

They're almost in the middle when a bullet hits the road ...

carrying a lot of plastic bottles. Many people in Sarajevo look exactly the same. The men on the hills can kill him at any time. Kenan doesn't know why some people are shot and not others. How do they choose? Why haven't they chosen him?

He walks between buildings which have four or five floors of flats. Shells have hit most of the buildings, but people are still living there. This part of the city isn't as bad as others.

A green Volkswagen car is in front of one of the buildings. A shell has made a large hole in it. Kenan thinks he knows the owner of the car. Last time they met, the man didn't say anything about it. But these days, it's not unusual enough to bring into a conversation.

Kenan passes a building on his left. Before the war it was a supermarket, but now it's a centre for food and other help from foreign countries. He walks to the door, but it's closed. This means there's no free food. There hasn't been any foreign help for weeks – maybe more than a month.

Kenan turns back to the street. He sees a man that he knows, a soldier. It's his friend Ismet. Ismet worked as a taxi driver before he joined the army at the start of the war. Usually, he's at the front line of the fighting for four days, then he has four days at home with his wife and baby daughter. Sometimes, late at night, he comes to Kenan's house and tells him about the fighting. The stories are terrible.

One night, Ismet and a friend had one gun and twenty bullets between them. They had to defend their position against enemy soldiers. They knew that it wasn't possible. They waited all night and were very frightened, but nothing happened. When morning came, they were both very happy. They were alive! Later that day, a shell landed close to them and Ismet's friend died. When Ismet tells Kenan the story, he laughs a little. Kenan can't understand why.

'We lived through the night,' Ismet says. 'That was all

that we hoped for. We were given that, and we were happy. It didn't matter how much longer we lived after that. A few hours, or fifty years, it was the same.'

Kenan doesn't want to join the army. He hopes that he won't have to. He's afraid of dying, and that is part of a soldier's job. But he's more afraid of killing. For Kenan, it's an impossible idea. He's never talked to Ismet about that.

Ismet looks tired. His green jacket is dirty and he hasn't shaved. But he smiles when he sees Kenan. Kenan is happy to see him.

'Any news?' Ismet asks, pointing to the food centre.

'No – and I was hoping for a nice steak today,' Kenan jokes.

Ismet hands him a cigarette. Kenan knows that it's probably Ismet's last packet. He doesn't want to take it.

'Have one. I've got more,' says Ismet.

The two men stand in the street, smoking their cigarettes. It's good to be together for a few minutes. Then Ismet turns to go.

'Good luck with your water. I'll visit you tonight or tomorrow.'

Kenan continues along the street. He passes buildings with broken windows and holes in the walls. Some are ruins. At the end of this street is a bus stop. It's where Kenan caught his bus to work. The buses haven't run anywhere in the city since one was hit by a shell. Kenan saw that bus soon after it happened. Thick, black smoke filled the air. A lot of people died in the explosion. For Kenan, the war won't be at an end until the buses run again.

If he turns left, he'll come to the marketplace. There's usually food there, but the prices are very high. Most people in Sarajevo don't have enough money to buy it. Last month, Kenan sold his washing machine to buy food. Without electricity they couldn't use it, but he didn't get much money for it. There was enough for a bag of apples, a few kilos of potatoes and some bread and coffee.

He knows that some people don't have this problem. They drive around in new Mercedes cars and have plenty of food. He isn't sure how they do it. But there are stories in Sarajevo. People say that there's a tunnel under the airport. It's open twenty-four hours a day. But to use it you need to know someone important in the government. Kenan thinks that this explains the fat, rich men in Mercedes.

He has to cross the river to get to the brewery. Today, he decides to try the Princip Bridge. He passes the ruins of the Hotel Europa. He thinks about the end of the war, and about re-building Sarajevo. Who will do it? How will it look? He tries to imagine sitting in a coffee bar with friends. Will he ever feel comfortable and safe again? Kenan doesn't know, but he wants to try.

He's almost at the bridge when a man comes running around the corner.

'Sniper,' he says, pointing to the bridge. 'They're firing along the left side of the river.'

'I'm trying for the brewery,' says Kenan.

'It's safer at the Sĕher Cehaja.'

The Sĕher Cehaja is the most eastern bridge. It will double his trip if he crosses there. He thinks about the two kilometres more that he'll have to walk. Suddenly, a shell explodes a few streets away. Kenan makes his decision. He turns away from the Princip Bridge and walks east.

He has to go past a large square with shops on each side. These shops are all closed now; nobody has money in Sarajevo. In the middle of the square are some seats and a small garden. In the past, people met their friends here. Now, it's not a good place to be. The men in the hills can easily see people in the square, so only birds stay there now.

Kenan walks close to the buildings. Suddenly, he hears a noise from one of the birds and watches it move past him. The bird isn't walking or flying, but it's moving quickly along the ground. It disappears into the doorway of a building. Then the same thing happens again and Kenan understands. Someone is fishing for birds.

He steps closer to the door and sees an old man sitting there. The man waves to Kenan. He's holding a stick, with some thin rope tied to it. He ties a piece of bread to the rope, then he throws it out into the square. A bird looks interested. The man waits. Finally, the bird decides. It moves closer and then eats the bread in one bite. It looks pleased. It's found a small meal. The man pulls the stick and the bird is pulled hard from inside. It jumps into the air and tries to fly, but it can't escape. The bird is pulled into the doorway and the man kills it. He puts it into a bag.

'Sometimes they try to fly, sometimes they don't,' he says. 'I don't understand what makes a difference.'

'Have you been lucky today?' Kenan asks.

'Yes, I've got six. That's one for every person in my flat,' the man replies. 'I don't take more than I need. Then I hope there'll be some for tomorrow.'

The old man takes his bag of dead birds and walks away.

It's a good way to feed a family. But Kenan feels a little sorry for the birds.

The men on the hills are doing the same to us, he thinks. They kill a few each day so there will always be more the next day.

◆

Arrow's commander has called her into his office. Nermin Filipović is a good-looking man in his late thirties, with dark hair and a small beard. He was a professional soldier before the war. Only a few officers like Nermin left Europe's fourth-largest army to defend Sarajevo. If the men on the hills ever get into the city, they will kill these officers first.

'We have a special job for you,' he says. 'An important job.'

Until now, Arrow has been able to make her own decisions. She's chosen who to kill, when and how. But she knew that would change one day.

'I'd like you to think about our first conversation,' she says.

At the start of the war, Nermin needed snipers to defend the city. He talked to everyone in the university shooting team. Arrow was the best in the team.

'I've never shot at a person,' she said then. 'I don't want to kill people.'

'You'll save lives,' he said. 'They'll try to kill us all.'

Arrow thought about this. She thought about sending a bullet into a person and not a piece of paper. She was surprised that it didn't worry her so much. She thought that she could probably do it. She thought she could live with it too.

'I think this will end,' she said. 'And then I want to go back to the life that I had before. I want my hands to be clean. If I do this, I'll do it my way. I won't kill on your orders.'

So they agreed. Arrow worked alone and she made her own decisions. She reported only to Nermin. This was how it was, until today.

Nermin remembers that conversation. He stands up and opens the door. Then he tells her to follow him.

'I have something to show you,' he says. 'Don't worry, your hands will stay clean.'

They walk through the city streets.

'Wait,' he says. He looks at his watch. 'It's almost time.'

Soon they're standing in front of a shop in the heart of the city, across from the market. Arrow knows this street. She knows that a few days ago a shell exploded here. Many people died while they waited for bread.

Nermin looks at his watch. 'It's time,' he says. 'Here he comes.'

A tall man with black hair, a moustache and a sad face walks into the street. He's wearing a tuxedo and carrying a cello under one arm. In the other hand he has a chair. He walks into the middle of the street, sits down and places the cello between his legs.

'What's he doing?' Arrow asks, but Nermin says nothing.

The cellist closes his eyes. When he opens them again, the sad look on his face has gone. His left hand holds the neck of the cello, his right hand lifts the bow, and he starts to play.

It's the most beautiful music that Arrow has ever heard. She stands against the wall, but she isn't really there. She closes her eyes and pictures from her past come into her head.

She's a child again. Her mother lifts her up. She's running through a field with her dog. She tastes snow on her tongue, then feels the sun on her face. Her first boyfriend kisses her.

You will not cry, she tells herself. But the music is doing strange things to her. She feels sad and happy at the same time. She tries very hard to stay calm. And then the cellist finishes playing. He picks up his chair and his cello and walks inside.

Nermin is looking at her.

'We need you to keep him alive,' he says.

'I don't understand.'

'He's said that he will do this every day for twenty-two days,' Nermin replies. 'This is the eighth day. People see him. The world has seen him. He mustn't die.'

Arrow looks around.

'A sniper on the hills can't shoot him there,' she says. 'He's safe in the middle of these buildings. But perhaps they'll shell the street again.'

'No, they won't want to end it that way. We have

information,' says Nermin. 'We think the enemy will send a sniper into this part of the city. That's how they'll kill him. We need you to protect him.'

Arrow isn't sure she can do this.

'Things are changing on our side,' says Nermin. 'I don't know how much longer you'll be able to work alone ...'

'But we agreed!' says Arrow.

'I know. And if you can do this, it will be easier for both of us.'

Nermin turns and walks away. Arrow stands for a few more minutes. Then she hears a shell fall in another part of the city. She pulls her coat tightly around her shoulders and starts to walk home.

Chapter 3 Old Friends, New Enemies

Maybe the sniper has gone. He hasn't fired for ten minutes. Since then, a few people have crossed without a problem. Dragan moves closer to the crossing. He's hungry now and the bakery is quite close. There are only two more dangerous crossroads and then he'll be there. But he doesn't have to hurry. It's better to be careful.

He steps away from the crossing and stands close to a broken old lorry. Here, he's protected from snipers in the hills at Vraca. In the past, he took his wife and son up there sometimes in the summer. From there, you could see most of the city below. It's a view that the snipers like.

He looks to his right and sees a woman coming towards him. As she gets closer, he sees her more clearly. It's Emina, a friend of his wife. Dragan has always liked her, but not her husband, Jovan. He looks down at his shoes. He hopes she'll walk straight past. But Emina has already seen him.

'Dragan, is that you?' Emina's hand touches his shoulder. He looks up at her and smiles. She smiles back. She's wearing a blue wool coat that he remembers. His wife liked it. Dragan wanted to buy one for her, but he never did.

'How are you? How's Raza? Where are you staying?'

Dragan answers her questions. He'd like to tell her about his feelings when Raza and their son left Sarajevo. He'd like to tell her about the night when his flat was destroyed. But he can't. If he does, they'll be there for days. There is too much to tell.

Emina knows there is more. But she doesn't ask. She waits for him to speak. Finally, he does.

'How's Jovan?'

'He joined the army. I don't see much of him.'

Dragan is surprised. He thought that Jovan was more of a talker than a fighter. He isn't sure what to say to this.

'There's a sniper firing on this crossing,' he says. 'I'm waiting until it's safe.'

'I'm not in a hurry,' says Emina. 'I'm taking some medicine to an address near the bakery. It was my mother's, and she died five years ago. But it's probably still OK.'

They talk about people that they both know. Most of them didn't leave Sarajevo at the start of the war. Now they can't leave. The only way out is through the tunnel.

'I don't have friends in the government, or lots of money,' says Dragan, 'so I can't leave now.'

'Why didn't you go with Raza?'

'I wanted to protect our flat, and to keep my job. Maybe I made a mistake.'

'No, we must stay. If we all go, they'll come down from the hills. Then the city will be theirs.'

'If we stay, they will kill us all. So the result will be the same – the city will be theirs.'

'The world is looking at Sarajevo. They'll have to help us.'

'Nobody is coming,' says Dragan. 'We're alone here.'

Emina puts her hands in the pockets of her coat.

'I know that nobody is coming,' she says quietly. 'But I don't want to believe it.'

Dragan doesn't want to believe it, either. The men on the hills are winning. They're taking his life away from him. He needs to keep some control over it, so he makes a decision.

'I think I'll cross now,' he says to her.

'OK,' she says. 'I'll follow after you.'

Dragan moves towards the road. He starts to run.

He feels the bullet passing before he hears it. It flies past his left ear. Then he hears the shot. He stands, surprised. Then he turns and runs back towards Emina. He thinks he hears her calling his name. His shoulder hits the metal of an old lorry and he tries not to fall. This is the first time that a sniper has shot at him. He's lucky to be alive.

'Are you hurt?' Emina asks him.

'No,' says Dragan. 'For a sniper, he's not a very good shot.'

She puts her hand on his back and they both laugh.

♦

Arrow dresses in silence, picks up her rifle and closes the door to her flat. It's early morning and the streets are almost empty. This is Arrow's favourite time of day. There are no shells. She can almost imagine that there is no war.

She returns to the street that she was in yesterday. She stands in the same place, with her back to the wall. Then she crosses the street. She sits where the cellist sat. She knows that twenty-two people died here. Many more were badly hurt. They made a small decision — to buy bread. Arrow understands now that life is like this. It's one small decision after another. Firing a bullet, crossing a road, buying bread.

She doesn't understand the cellist. Why is he doing this? Is he crazy? She doesn't think so.

I will keep this man alive, she thinks. *He will finish the twenty-two days.* She doesn't understand him. But Arrow knows this is important.

She looks up at the buildings opposite. There's no glass in the windows, only plastic. She thinks about the snipers in the hills. They will send a man in to shoot the cellist from one of these buildings. And the sniper will want to escape when he's finished. So Arrow thinks about the best way to escape. Suddenly, she realises. There's only one area that he will use.

Arrow walks towards the buildings that the shot will come from. The sniper will know that she's waiting for him. She looks for a hiding-place, so she can kill him. If he sees her, his first shot will kill her. Then he will kill the cellist.

She smiles. She has a plan.

Hours later, Arrow sits in a room on the south side of the street. She's cut a hole in the plastic at the window. Through this, she will be able to see the sniper. It's the perfect place.

She watches the street and the buildings for hours. When something changes, she'll know. There are three windows which interest her. Arrow believes that the sniper will shoot from one of those windows.

The cellist walks into the street. He sits down and starts playing. Arrow looks closely at the three windows. Suddenly, she sees a hole in the plastic at one of them. It's a window on the fourth floor. She looks down to the street.

Two young girls are standing in front of the cellist. If the sniper shoots now, he'll kill one or all of them. The girls put some flowers at the feet of the cellist. Then they turn and walk away from him.

Arrow looks at the fourth floor window again. Something moves and she sees a shadow behind the plastic. She waits for him to show himself. Ten minutes pass. Nothing changes. She

He waits close to a wall and looks up at the hills.

looks down to the street. She sees that the cellist has gone.

Why didn't the sniper shoot? Why wait for another day? Arrow doesn't understand. But she hasn't failed in her job. The cellist is alive and he'll be there tomorrow. Arrow will be there too.

♦

Kenan looks at the ruins of the National Library. It was one of his favourite places in the city. Now everything inside the building is destroyed. Shells exploded on the building and it burned for hours. Blackened pieces of a million books fell onto Sarajevo for days after that.

He walks around the corner and sees the Sěher Ćehaja Bridge in front of him. He waits close to a wall and looks up at the hills. He can't see anyone, but they're there. He knows that. If they're looking, they can see him.

A man and a woman come around the corner. They walk towards the bridge and start to cross. They walk a little faster, but neither of them runs. They reach the middle of the bridge and Kenan waits for the sound of shots. But nothing happens and the two people reach the other side.

A woman arrives, carrying two water containers.

'Is it safe?' she asks Kenan.

'Two people have just crossed. Are you going to the brewery? Do you want to cross together?'

The woman thinks about this.

'No,' she says. 'I'm going to wait a little longer.'

So Kenan steps out into the street alone. He moves as quickly as he can. His feet hit the bridge. He knows that he's in the most dangerous place now. He runs to the left, then to the right. He runs faster. The water containers crash against his legs. He's very frightened. Then he reaches the end of the bridge and runs to a small building on his left.

He sits there for a few minutes until he's calm again. He looks back at the woman on the other side of the bridge. She's still waiting. Then he understands why. Kenan was her test. In the same way, he used the man and woman before him. Everyone is testing the snipers.

It's time to continue. The brewery isn't far now, just up another hill. As Kenan gets closer, he sees water running down the street. A lorry comes towards him. On the back is a very large plastic water container. There are many more people in the street here with water bottles. They all have to stand to one side so the lorry can get past them. Other lorries follow.

Then the red building of the brewery comes into view. Kenan feels both happy and worried. Finally he's arrived. But it's a long way home.

Chapter 4   One Dead Sniper

'I don't understand how you're not afraid,' Dragan says to Emina. 'You're putting your life in danger on the road, but this medicine is years out of date.'

'There's a man playing the cello in the street,' Emina says. 'Near the market. Where people died in the line for bread.'

Dragan knows about the explosion near the market, but he hasn't thought about it since then. People die every day.

'Every day, at four o'clock,' Emina continues, 'he sits there and plays. People go and listen. Some leave flowers. I've been there many times. Sometimes I listen until the end, and sometimes I only stay for a few minutes.'

Dragan has heard about the cellist. He doesn't understand why Emina is telling him this. But he doesn't stop her.

'Why do you think he's doing this?' she asks. 'Is he playing for the people who died? Or is he playing for the people who haven't?'

He can see that she wants an answer. He doesn't have one.

'Who's he playing for?' Emina asks again.

Suddenly, Dragan thinks that he knows. 'Maybe he's playing for himself,' he says. 'Maybe it's all that he can do.'

'I'm afraid of everything, Dragan,' she says quietly. 'Of dying and of not dying. I'm afraid that this war isn't a war. It's how life will always be now.'

'I know,' he says.

They stand together, in silence.

'I'll go now,' says Emina. 'Maybe I'll get back in time to hear the cellist.'

'I'll go with you,' says Dragan. But when they reach the road, he stops. He puts his hand on Emina's arm.

'I can't go yet,' he says. 'I'm not ready.'

Two people are crossing from the other side. The man is wearing a brown hat. He's almost halfway across the road. Emina steps into the street and runs. A young man starts to cross behind her. Suddenly, Emina is thrown to one side and there's the sound of a rifle shot. Emina lies, unmoving, on the road. Dragan can't see if she's alive or not.

The young man runs to Emina. He reaches her at the same time as the man with the hat. The young man puts his arms around her and lifts her up. The man in the hat doesn't stop – he runs past. As he passes, the young man shouts to him for help.

When the man in the hat is almost safe, there's another shot. The hat flies off his head and lands at Dragan's feet. The man is lying on his stomach in the road.

The young man is carrying Emina towards Dragan. Dragan can see now that she's alive. Her blue coat is red with blood from her arm. As they pass the hatless man, he reaches a hand up to them. The young man doesn't stop. A bullet hits the road a metre in front of them.

Emina and the young man reach Dragan and fall onto the ground next to him. Emina cries out, but Dragan is looking at the hatless man. He's trying to pull himself along the street towards them. Then there's another rifle shot and the man's head explodes.

Dragan is holding the man's hat, but he doesn't remember picking it up. He puts it down on the street, and then turns to Emina.

♦

It's nearly nine in the morning. Arrow is sitting again in the place where the cellist will play. She's tired. She looks up at the fourth floor window. She's sure that the sniper will be there later. Then she realises that he's there now. He's watching her. Does he know why she's here? Arrow doesn't think so. She puts her hands in her pockets and walks away slowly. She doesn't look back.

Later, she looks down into the street from her hiding-place. It's almost time for the cellist to walk out of his building. She gets her rifle ready and looks along it. She points it towards the fourth floor window. The cellist begins to play.

After five minutes, Arrow knows that something is wrong. Then she sees a movement in a different window. She knows he's found her. She jumps quickly to one side as a bullet shoots through the plastic at her window. It hits the wall behind her. Arrow waits for a second shot, but there isn't one. The cellist plays to the end of the piece. For some reason, the sniper hasn't shot him. Arrow doesn't move. She wants him to believe that she's dead.

Later, in Nermin's office, she tells him what happened.

'I'll put a man in there tonight,' he says. 'Maybe the sniper will go looking for a body.'

The cellist begins to play.

Arrow thinks that Nermin looks tired.

'I know I've made promises to you,' he says. 'But things are changing. It's going to be difficult for both of us in the next few days.'

He stands up, and Arrow leaves the office.

The next day, she returns to the same building. This time, she uses the room next door. At four o'clock, the cellist comes out and Arrow gets ready. She sees the sniper immediately. He's in another of the three windows that she saw that first day.

The cellist starts to play. The sniper moves closer to the window. Arrow is ready to send a bullet into him. But then she stops. The sniper's left hand isn't on the rifle. It's hanging at his side. He lifts his head. She sees that his eyes are closed. It's clear that he's listening to the music. Now she knows why he didn't fire yesterday.

Arrow knows that she doesn't want to kill this man. She also knows that she must. He's probably killed hundreds of people. She must kill him now. There isn't much time.

The music comes to an end and the sniper smiles. He opens his eyes and Arrow fires. The man falls and the rifle falls on top of him.

The cellist picks up his chair and his cello, and walks towards his door. He stops at the entrance. Arrow hopes that he will look towards her. But he doesn't. He disappears into the building.

♦

Shells have hit the brewery many times and the building isn't safe. But the water is brought up from streams deep down below its floor, so the men on the hills can't reach the pipes with their shells. Outside, there are about a hundred people waiting in line for water. Kenan has been here when there were three times as many. He's happy that he won't have to wait for hours today.

More pipes carry the water up to the street. People try to fill their containers as quickly as they can. But there's also time for conversation. It's good to be out with other people.

The woman in front of Kenan finishes and he steps forward to the pipe. He takes the tops off his containers and puts them carefully on the ground. His bottles are in a line on his left. He picks up the first bottle and holds it under the cold water. When it's full, he puts it on his right. Then, as quickly as possible, he takes the next container and fills it with water. He continues like this until all of them are full.

Suddenly, he hears the sound of a shell and it's very close. He knows that it's going to fall near him. The shell hits. It's the loudest sound that Kenan has ever heard. He's knocked off his feet by the explosion. Then there's a second shell. And then, silence.

He can't move at first. He sees people running past him, down the street. Slowly, he sits up. He finds that he isn't hurt. He's sitting in a pool of water, but his bottles haven't fallen. They're still standing, and full.

He looks around. The shells exploded about thirty metres away, at the end of the line of people. He stands and walks towards the place. There are many dead bodies, and people crying for help. Men start to put people into a car at the end of the street. All around him men and women are screaming, running and shouting. Kenan can't do anything to help. He looks down at his feet. He's only a few metres from the place where the first shell exploded. Around it, the ground is dark red, but here it's clean. Water is running from the brewery pipes and making a clear river in the centre of the road.

Kenan walks up the hill again to his containers. At the top of the street an old car takes more people away to the hospital. At the side of the road there are about seven bodies. A blue vehicle arrives and four men get out. Together they lift the bodies into the back and then drive away.

Kenan puts the tops on his six containers, pulls the rope through the handles and starts the walk down the hill. He goes past the place where the first shell fell, then the second. He doesn't stop or look at the ground. There's nothing more to see. At the bottom of the street he stops. He has to decide which bridge to cross. Shells are exploding everywhere. The weight of the bottles will make it difficult for him to run.

He can wait for the shelling to stop, but maybe this will take hours. Or he can cross at the Ćumurija Bridge. This will be difficult because the bridge is almost in ruins. He will probably have to make two trips to get all his containers across. But it's better than waiting for hours. He wants to be home again.

He reaches a crossroads. He moves across it as fast as he can. When he gets to the bridge, he sees a man starting to cross from the other side. He doesn't think that they can pass on the narrow bridge. He decides to take all his containers in one trip. They're heavy, but with three on each side he can do it.

The man reaches Kenan's side of the bridge. Kenan starts to cross. He has to stop after every few steps because the containers are moving too much. He gets to the middle of the bridge, stops again and then continues. He's near the end of the bridge when he almost falls. The water containers crash into the metal at the side of the bridge. As he stands straight again, the containers hit him on the legs. He shakes with fear. Then he suddenly feels very angry. He runs to the end of the bridge, drops his water containers and throws himself onto the ground. He screams. Then he turns onto his back and looks at the sky.

He's tired. He's tired from getting water. He's tired of the world that he lives in. He didn't want this world and he didn't help to make it. He wants a different life.

Slowly, Kenan gets up off the ground. He picks up the rope and lifts his water bottles again. He takes one step, then another. Soon he will be home.

Chapter 5 Time to Disappear

There's a small group of people around Emina. They've taken her coat off and someone hands it to Dragan. The bullet hit the top of her arm and there's a lot of blood, but it doesn't look too bad. There's the sound of gunfire somewhere in the city.

Emina looks up at Dragan and smiles.

'He's a better shot than we thought,' she says.

'It's a good thing that he's not better. You're lucky.'

'I wanted to see the cellist today.'

A car comes along the street. A few of the group run towards it and wave. Emina sounds sleepy now.

'Jovan will be angry with me. He doesn't like me to go out. But I can't be a prisoner in my own home. I had to get outside and walk around.'

'Jovan will be fine. You'll be fine too,' Dragan says. He's watching the car coming towards them. When he looks at Emina again, her eyes are closed.

Two men get out of the car and run to them. They look at the hatless man, but they can do nothing for him. They pick Emina up and place her on the back seat of the car. Then they jump in the car and drive away.

'She'll be OK,' one of the group says to Dragan. 'They'll look after her at the hospital.'

Dragan sits with his back against an old lorry. He still holds Emina's coat. He feels something in the pocket, and takes it out. It's her dead mother's medicine, and an address. He puts them in his own pocket. She won't want the blue coat now.

It only needs washing and mending. But Dragan knows that she'll never want to wear it again.

He didn't try to help Emina and he feels bad about it. He didn't help the young man carry her off the road. When the sniper fired, he didn't move. He was too frightened.

Dragan looks southwest, where the bakery is. If he continues walking, past the bakery, he'll come to Dobrinja. This is where the tunnel under the airport starts. He imagines himself handing a note to the guard at the entrance. It's his permission to use the tunnel. He goes past the guard and into the tunnel. It's low and narrow and there's water on the ground. As he reaches the end, it gets wider and higher. The air is fresher. When he comes out, he's only eight kilometres from his sister's house. But he's free. Two hours on a bus, then a boat trip and he's in Italy.

His wife and son will be very happy to see him. He'll have a hot shower, and then they'll go to a restaurant. He'll be able to choose his meal. They'll walk through the streets together and nobody will shoot at them. They will hate nobody and nobody will hate them.

In the hills behind him, a shell explodes. Then there's the sound of gunfire. He's back in Sarajevo again. There's no note in his pocket, and there never will be. Nobody is getting out of Sarajevo now.

Dragan doesn't want to go to Italy. He misses his wife and son, but he isn't Italian. This is his home. This is where he wants to be. He wants all the things that he imagined in Italy. But Dragan wants them here in Sarajevo. He still has hope.

He will never forget what happened here. If the siege ends, he won't be able to explain it. How was it possible? Dragan doesn't know. He can't believe that it's happened. He hopes he never will be able to.

◆

Arrow sits in Nermin's office. She waits for half an hour before he arrives. He looks like he hasn't slept for days.

'It's done,' she says. 'He's dead.'

'Which one?' Nermin asks. 'The cellist or the sniper?'

'The sniper.'

'Good.' An assistant brings in some coffee, then leaves. Arrow says nothing.

'Maybe you've done this for long enough,' Nermin says. 'Maybe you should stop now.'

Arrow looks down at the floor.

'The sniper was ready to shoot. But he didn't. He was listening to the cellist play.'

'No, you don't understand me.'

'I killed him because he shot at me. I couldn't leave him there. I had to do it.'

'Yes, you did. But this has nothing to do with the cellist. It's time for you to disappear.'

Arrow looks up at him. 'Disappear?'

'I can't protect you now,' he says.

Where, she thinks, can I disappear to? I can't get out of the city.

'The men on the hills are terrible people,' Nermin says. 'But there are worse men here in the city. They're using the war and this city to make their own lives better. Some are making money from it. I don't agree with it.'

Arrow has heard many stories. She doesn't know what to believe.

'What are they doing?' she asks.

'You should disappear now. Then you won't find out.'

'What will happen to you?'

'They'll take me away. That will happen very soon.'

He comes out from behind his desk and kisses her. Nermin

has been a friend to Arrow. She's sad to say goodbye to him.

She walks out of his office into the bright light of the street. Her rifle feels heavy on her shoulder. She doesn't know what will happen to Nermin. Maybe he can leave the city. Maybe he can hide until the war ends.

Soon, the shelling starts again. People start to move faster. A boy runs past Arrow and knocks into her shoulder. He turns and looks at her. She sees that it's Nermin's assistant. His face is white and he looks very frightened. He runs away, fast.

Arrow stops. Something's wrong. She turns around and starts walking back towards Nermin's office. She walks faster until she's running. She sees the building at the end of the street. And then there's a great explosion and the doors fly off into the street. A ball of fire follows.

Arrow knows immediately that there was only one person in the building.

The fire fighters arrive and put out the fire. She hears them talking together. They all know that this wasn't a shell, but an explosion from inside. She waits for hours. Finally, two soldiers come out of the building with a body. It's covered with a coat. Arrow knows it's Nermin. She puts her rifle on her shoulder and starts the long walk home.

Later, Arrow lies in bed, thinking. 'Disappear,' Nermin told her. The army pays her in cigarettes. Has she got enough cigarettes to buy her way through the tunnel? But then she remembers the cellist. He hasn't finished yet, and they may send another sniper. She wants to protect him.

She wakes to the sound of boots on the stairs. There are men outside her room. Somebody knocks hard on the door. She pulls on her clothes and opens it.

Three men with guns wait on the other side of the door.

'Are you Arrow?' the first asks.

'Possibly. What do you want?'

And then there's a great explosion ...

'Come with us.'

'Where are we going?' she asks.

'To see Edin Karaman,' he says. 'Bring your rifle.'

Arrow has never heard of Karaman and that makes her nervous. She gets her rifle from the kitchen and they leave together. One man walks next to her, the other two behind. She feels like a prisoner.

They take Arrow to a café in a narrow street near the library. At the back of the empty room, a man is sitting at a table. He looks hard – a soldier and a fighter. Arrow can see that he's a dangerous man. She doesn't want him as her enemy.

'Sit,' he says. 'And leave your rifle by the door. My name is Edin Karaman and I'm your new commander. You are Arrow?'

'Yes.'

'And what's your real name?'

'Arrow is my only name now,' she says.

He looks at some papers on the table and lights a cigarette.

'It's not important. You are now under my control.'

'What about Nermin Filipović?'

'He's dead, as you know.' He looks up at her. 'You're very good with a rifle.'

'What do you want from me?'

'I want you to continue as a sniper,' he says. 'But I'll give you your orders now and you will report to me.'

'No,' says Arrow. 'That's not how I work.'

'You don't understand me. I'm not asking you, I'm ordering you. We're at war. You will do as you are told.'

'I have a job already. I must finish it.'

'The cellist is not your problem now. We've given that job to another gunman.'

'Why?'

'Because I say so. Filipović didn't make good use of you. That cellist is nothing.' Edin Karaman stands. 'You will go with

34

the men outside. They'll take you to meet someone. He's the man you will work with. He'll tell you about your next job.'

Arrow doesn't move. 'I work alone,' she says. 'I choose who and when I kill.'

'No, you don't. I make the decisions, not you. Now go.'

Arrow isn't sure what to do. There's nothing more that she can say to this man. She stands and turns towards the door.

'One last thing,' he calls. Arrow turns to face him. 'There's nothing difficult about this war. But some people have a problem understanding it. So I'm going to explain it to you now. There is us, and there is them. Everyone, and I mean everyone, is in one of these two groups. Do you know which group you're in? I hope so.' Then he waves her away.

Arrow picks up her rifle. If he wants her to kill the men on the hills, she'll do it. There is nothing more that she can do.

Chapter 6 Right and Wrong

Kenan is on his way home when he sees Ismet again. Ismet smiles.

'What took you so long?' he asks.

Kenan doesn't smile. He isn't sure what to say. 'There was shelling at the brewery.'

The smile leaves Ismet's face. 'Are you OK?' he asks.

'I'm fine,' he says. But he isn't fine. He knows that Ismet can see this. But he doesn't want to talk about it now.

'Come with me to the market,' Ismet says.

The market is busy. It's difficult for Kenan to walk through the crowd with all his water containers.

'Wait here,' Ismet says. 'If there's anything good for sale, I'll tell you.'

Ismet disappears into the crowd. This isn't the most

expensive market. But Kenan knows that many of the things here are selling for crazy prices. He thinks about the tunnel. Why don't they use it to get all the children out of Sarajevo? But Kenan knows the answer already. The tunnel is used to bring in the things in this market. And then he suddenly understands what happened to his washing machine. Cars come through the tunnel with things to sell. And they don't return empty. Someone, in another city far away, has bought a cheap washing machine.

He sees a man standing next to a black Mercedes. The man is wearing a new suit and looks well-fed. He's smoking a cigarette and he's looking towards Kenan. A lorry drives past. It's one of the lorries that he saw at the brewery. It stops behind the black Mercedes and the driver gets out. He talks to the man in the suit. The man hands the driver a piece of paper. The driver gets back into the lorry and drives away.

Kenan understands what's happened. They're buying and selling water. And now he's angry. He'd like to hit the man in the suit. He'd like to kill him. Kenan steps forward and starts moving towards him, slowly at first. He gets faster and tries running, but it's difficult with his water.

The man throws the rest of his cigarette onto the ground and gets into the Mercedes. He puts on a pair of sunglasses, starts the car and moves away. He's disappeared before Kenan gets close to him. An old woman picks up the half cigarette from the side of the road and hurries away.

Kenan hears music playing softly. He can only hear it when the street is quiet. He doesn't know why, but he starts to follow the sound. The music gets louder. He turns a corner and sees a crowd of people. They're all looking at something. He finds a place to stand. Then he puts his water bottles down.

Kenan knows this man. He's seen him play before, but he can't remember where. The man's tuxedo is dirty, his

hair is untidy and he hasn't shaved for many days. There a
large dark circles under his eyes. Kenan has heard the cellist'.
story. Someone, maybe Ismet, maybe his wife, told him. The
cellist saw the explosion from his window and now he plays
here every day. When Kenan first heard about it, he didn't
understand. He thought it was silly. Why was the cellist doing
it? It wasn't helping anyone.

But now, as he listens, none of this matters. Kenan starts to
feel better as the music reaches inside him. He stops feeling
angry. The cellist begins to look different. His dirty tuxedo
becomes clean, his shoes shine like mirrors. The man's hair is
smooth and his beard disappears.

The building behind the cellist is not a ruin. The people in
the street stand up taller. Their faces put on weight and colour.
Sarajevo is, again, the city that he grew up in.

Kenan imagines going home to his flat. He'll kiss Amila and
the family will go out to a restaurant in town. They'll come
home on the bus, happy and full of food. The people around
them will have nothing to worry about. Kenan will look at his
wife and children and he'll be happy. Nothing can take that
away from him.

But then it is all taken away. The music stops. He is back on
the street. Twenty-two people died here, while buying bread.

The cellist picks up his chair and his cello and disappears
into a building. Some people have left flowers in the street.
Slowly, everyone leaves until only Kenan and an old woman
are left.

The woman is looking at the pile of flowers and at the hole
in the road. She turns to Kenan.

'My daughter,' she says, 'was here to buy bread. She didn't
need any. I asked her to get me some.'

Kenan doesn't know what to say to her,

'One day my grandchildren will ask how their mother died.

hat shall I tell them?'

Kenan has no answer for her. They stand together and look at the flowers.

'Did your daughter like the cello?' Kenan asks.

'I don't know. She never said so.'

'I think she was a great lover of music,' he says. He's suddenly sure of it.

The old woman turns and looks at him. She smiles a small smile, then walks away.

Kenan stays a little longer, then picks up his water and goes back to the market. He sees Ismet across the street. Ismet is talking to a man. He puts three packets of cigarettes on the table. They talk some more. Finally, the man takes the cigarettes and gives Ismet some money. Kenan watches Ismet take the money to a woman in the market. He uses it to buy a small bag of rice.

Kenan knows that this is foreign food – free food. It was sent to Sarajevo to help them. It's against the law to sell it. But he knows it happens. The cigarettes were Ismet's army pay. He earned them trying to keep the people of Sarajevo safe. Kenan has just watched his friend buy free rice with his army pay.

There is the sound of shooting from Grbavica. Kenan hears shelling in the west, near the airport.

He sees Ismet walk out of the market. Ismet won't find Kenan. He'll think that he went home, tired. Later, he'll come to the flat and they'll joke together and talk about their families. And they'll hope for this to end. One day, they will help to rebuild Sarajevo.

Kenan turns towards home. He wants to get there before dark.

♦

They take Arrow to the Parliament building. It was one of the tallest buildings in the city. The men on the hills have hit the top floors with hundreds of shells and much of it has burned.

A man is waiting for her on the ground floor. There are two guards at the entrance, but they don't look at her. The three men with Arrow leave.

'I'm Hasan,' the man says. 'I've heard about you. They say that you're good at your job. It'll be nice to work with you.'

They walk up fourteen floors in silence. When they come into a room, there's a lot of broken glass and pieces of metal on the floor. The windows have all gone and there are great holes in the walls.

'Are you ready to go shooting?' he asks.

'No, I'm not,' Arrow replies. 'What are we doing here?'

'Karaman is testing you,' Hasan says. 'I'm going to choose someone, then you fire. Easy. You'll be fine.'

'Who are we shooting?'

'I don't know yet. Let's see who's out there.'

They go into another room and lie on their stomachs in front of the windows. It's not possible to get a good shot like that. If Arrow stands up, the men on the hills will see her. She points to a hole in the wall.

'That's a better position,' she says. She doesn't think Hasan will agree. She's surprised when he does.

They're looking down onto Grbavica. The enemy is in control here, but Arrow can't see any soldiers.

'There!' says Hasan. 'I've found one.'

She looks, but this man is old and he's wearing ordinary clothes.

'He's not a soldier,' she says. Another man takes a step into her line of fire. He moves like a soldier and he's smoking a cigarette. When he turns, she sees his rifle.

'There, to the south. There's a soldier.' She gets ready to fire.

'No,' says Hasan. 'Forget him. I chose the other man. You must shoot him.'

Arrow looks at Hasan. 'I'm not going to kill him,' she says. 'He's not carrying a gun and he's not a soldier. I can't kill ordinary people.'

'I'm telling you to kill him. This isn't a game. Other people can kill the soldiers. That isn't our job. Why do you think that man can walk around in Grbavica?'

Arrow knows the answer to that. It's because the men on the hills think of him as one of their own.

'He's not trying to kill us,' she says.

'It doesn't matter. He's one of them. They're his sons – he's their father, or grandfather, or uncle. There are two sides to this war, Arrow. Ours and theirs.' Hasan looks again down to the street. 'You can still get him,' he says. 'Take your shot.'

Arrow knows how she got here. The men on the hills hate her and now she hates them. It was an easy thing to do. Now she can't go back. She looks along her rifle at the old man in the street. But she sees the sniper who had to kill the cellist. His eyes are closed and he's listening. She hears the music again and this time she doesn't fire.

'No,' she says. 'I can't. It's wrong.'

Hasan doesn't move. 'Do you realise what you're doing?' he asks.

'I know exactly what I'm doing,' she says.

She walks away from Hasan and goes down to the ground floor. The guards at the entrance don't look at her as she leaves the building.

As she steps into the street, she checks her watch. It's almost four o'clock. Her feet hit the road and she begins to run.

♦

Dragan sees a foreign TV cameraman across the street. Maybe he wants to film the next person crossing. A young man gets ready to cross. He sees the cameraman too. It's clear that this crossing is dangerous. Nobody has moved the hatless man. Everyone can see him lying on the road. But this doesn't seem to worry the young man. He looks down and checks his clothes. Will he look good enough for TV? But the cameraman isn't ready to start filming yet. The young man makes a decision and starts his run. He's fast. Everyone watches. The sniper doesn't fire.

The cameraman is having a problem with his equipment. He looks in his bag and checks something on the camera. Dragan knows that the camera will start filming soon. He doesn't want the body of the hatless man to be filmed.

He wants people to know what's happening here. He wants reports from Sarajevo to go around the world. But the body of the hatless man won't say anything about what happened today. People won't know what this man was like. They won't understand his life. When they see his dead body on the evening news, they'll probably think nothing of it at all.

Dragan looks at the body of the hatless man. He doesn't know his name or anything about him. He can't picture his face. But it doesn't matter. This man is like him. He lived in this city under siege. He was shot crossing the street. They both did nothing when Emina needed help.

He remembers talking to Emina about the cellist: 'Maybe he's playing for himself. Maybe it's all that he can do.'

It doesn't matter what the world thinks of Sarajevo. But it matters what Dragan thinks. In the Sarajevo of his memory, it was completely wrong to leave a dead body in the street. In the Sarajevo of today, it's usual. That can't be right.

The hatless man is close, maybe fifteen metres from him. It's an easy run. Twenty steps each way.

Dragan is moving. He can hear his feet hitting the ground. His mouth feels dry. He keeps his head low as he runs. He reaches the body of the hatless man and takes one of his hands. He tries to take the other hand, but his shoe sticks in the man's blood and he falls. His nose is a centimetre from the dead man's head. But it doesn't matter now. He must get the body off the street.

Something hits the body in front of him. There's the sound of a rifle shot. Dragan tries to get to his feet and pull the man's body. He can't. The body's too heavy. He tries again and slowly he pulls it towards the side of the road.

He knows that the sniper will fire again. But now, Dragan isn't afraid. He hears another gunshot. He doesn't think that he's hurt. He pulls the body the final few steps – and then he's safe. He sits down on the ground and looks across the street. The cameraman is looking at him, his mouth open. His camera is in his hands, but not on his shoulder. He hasn't filmed Dragan, or the body of the hatless man.

Shells start to fall very near, and Dragan covers his head. There are more shots and then it's quiet again. He sits up. Will this ever end? Will people forget? He doesn't have the answers. When he gets to the bakery, he'll ask the other workers. They'll be surprised that he's talking to them again. He stands and picks up Emina's coat. Next to it is the man's hat, and he picks this up too.

When the people of Sarajevo can live happily with death, then the city will die. Then the men on the hills will win. Dragan takes Emina's coat, covers the man at his feet, and places the hat on top.

He pulls the body the final few steps – and then he's safe.

Chapter 7 The Last Day

Another day has just begun. Kenan is in his kitchen. He reaches for the plastic container with the last of the water. It's four days since he went to the brewery. Today's trip will be different, he knows. Today the cellist will play for the twenty-second and final time.

It's cold today. Kenan worries that the family won't have enough warm clothes for the winter. Where will he get wood for the fire? He doesn't know, but he'll find a way.

He checks his water containers. Then he gets ready to leave. Suddenly, the light in the kitchen comes on. They have electricity again – for a time. Amila comes into the kitchen and he points up at the light. She smiles.

'Do you think it will stay on for long?' she asks.

'Maybe.' Kenan ties up his water bottles.

'Be careful,' Amila says.

'Of course. I always am.'

'Bring me home a large box of chocolates,' she says, 'and twenty-four eggs.'

'Yes, OK. That's a lot of eggs,' says Kenan.

'I'm going to make a very large cake.'

Kenan kisses her and smiles. She puts her head on his shoulder.

'I'm tired,' she says quietly.

'I know,' he says. 'I'm tired too.'

After a minute or two, Kenan kisses her again and moves towards the door.

Outside the flat, he sits down on the steps and puts his head on his knees. He doesn't want to go out. He doesn't want to walk through the streets of his city. He doesn't want to see the ruins of buildings that he loved. He doesn't want to be in danger at every crossing. But he can't choose. He has to do it. He wants to be one of the people who rebuild Sarajevo. So he must go out into the streets and face the men on the hills. His family need water and he'll get it for them. There are many people in the city doing the same. They all find a way to continue with life.

Kenan has been to hear the cellist play every day since the shelling at the brewery. Every day, at four o'clock, he stands against a wall and watches the city come to life again. Today is the last day the cellist will play. He has played the Adagio for everyone who died in that attack. Nobody will play for the people who were killed at the brewery. Nobody will play for all the other people killed in Sarajevo, either. There aren't enough cellists in the city. But he's heard this cellist. It was enough.

Kenan steps out into the street. He starts his long walk down the hill, through the town, up the hill to the brewery and home again.

♦

Which is the real Sarajevo? Is it the city where people lived happily without war? Or is it the place that Dragan sees today? Is it the Sarajevo where people are trying to kill other people with bullets and shells?

It's past midday. Dragan has been at this crossing for more than two hours. It seems like days. He can cross any time he likes. Nobody has said that he can't. It's always been his decision.

He knows that the war will end one day. Then people will return to how they were before. He'll live in the real Sarajevo again. Until then, Dragan will walk the streets of this other Sarajevo. And he'll try to stop his city disappearing.

The cameraman has left and gone to a busier crossing. He needs to film people getting shot. If he waits long enough, he will.

Dragan makes up his mind. He's going across. The men on the hills aren't going to stop him. These are his streets. He'll walk them when he wants to. In a little less than four hours, the cellist will play for the final time.

There are clouds in the sky and it's getting colder. Somewhere, quite near, a car starts. A small bird flies overhead. Dragan isn't running. He knows that the sniper is probably watching the crossing. Just one shot, and he'll be dead.

His head tells him to run, but he can't. He walks across the road, past the place where Emina was shot, towards the other side. To someone watching, he looks like an old man out for a walk.

Dragan is very frightened, but he can't move faster. He stops trying. He keeps his eyes on the safe area that he's walking towards. He tries not to think about anything. He just puts one foot in front of the other.

He begins to understand why he isn't running. If he doesn't run, he's alive again. He wants to live in a Sarajevo that's alive again. If he runs, he's lost everything. It won't matter how many bodies lie in the streets.

Perhaps people will think that he's crazy. They're wrong. Dragan is awake again. He's been asleep since the war began. Now he thinks of Emina, trying to give her mother's medicine to a stranger. He thinks of the young man who saved her. And of the cellist who plays in the street.

He waits for gunfire, and the bullet that will hit him. But it never comes. He's both surprised and not surprised. It doesn't matter. If it comes, it will come. If it doesn't, he will be one of the lucky ones.

Dragan reaches the opposite side of the road. It's a good thing that the cameraman has gone. It wasn't good television. An old man walking across a street, with nothing happening. It's not really news.

He walks west towards the bakery. There, a small loaf of

bread waits for him. He'll be there in ten minutes. But then he puts his hand in his pocket. He finds the medicine and a piece of paper with an address on it. And then he knows that he'll be a little late at the bakery. But in half an hour he'll get his bread and he'll return this way. He doesn't think about the sniper now. On the way home, he'll go to a street south of the market. He'll wait for four o'clock. It's the cellist's last day. He wants to tell Emina what happened.

Dragan smiles as he passes an old man. The man keeps his eyes on the ground.

'Good afternoon,' Dragan says, brightly.

The man looks up. He seems surprised.

'Good afternoon,' Dragan repeats.

The man smiles and says the same to him.

♦

Arrow slept well. She didn't wake once in the night. Now she hears the sound of heavy boots coming up the stairs. She knew that they would come. Arrow opens her eyes. It's early in the morning, not quite seven o'clock. There's a gun on the table next to her bed, but she doesn't pick it up.

It's been ten days since she walked away from Hasan at the Parliament building. Ten days since she left Edin Karaman's team of killers. This is the first night, since then, that she's slept in her flat. They've found her already and Arrow is a little surprised.

They've searched for her for ten days. They knew that she was in one of the buildings above the cellist. But they couldn't find her. Karaman went there twice. He was in the line of her bullet, but she didn't shoot. She hasn't fired her rifle since she shot the sniper.

The cellist played for twenty-two days. This was what he promised. He was there every day at four o'clock in the afternoon. It didn't matter to him how much fighting there was. Some days people came to listen. Some days there was nobody there. He always played in the same way, except on the last day.

Arrow was in her hiding-place, watching. Nobody could see her. She felt the cellist come into the street. She knew that he was safe. The men on the hills weren't interested in him now. Her hand fell from her rifle. As the cellist began to play, she looked down into the street. It was full of people. Nobody moved.

Every note of the music reached into Arrow. She wanted to cry. The men on the hills didn't have to become killers. She didn't, either. But it happened. Nobody stopped it. There was so much hate in the city. But the music told a different story. There was hope for a better future.

Arrow closed her eyes. When she opened them, the music was finished. In the street, the cellist sat on his chair for a very long time. He was crying. One hand covered his face, the other held the cello. After a few minutes, he stood up and walked to the pile of flowers on the street. He looked at it, then he dropped his bow into the pile. Nobody in the street moved. They waited for him to say something. But he didn't speak. There was nothing for him to say. He turned, picked up his chair and went through the door to his flat. He didn't look back. Slowly people began to move away, until the street was empty.

The footsteps are at the top of the stairs now, just outside Arrow's door. She looks at her father's gun on the table next to her. If she uses it, the men outside the door will all die. It's the easiest decision in the world. Kill them and walk away.

But she isn't going to pick up the gun. She wants them to see it. But she chooses not to use it.

The men on the hills changed Arrow's life. Many things

were possible, before the war. But none of these things happened. She didn't get a good job, or a nice flat. She didn't spend evenings at the theatre with her friends. She didn't get married.

Now, nothing is possible. If she kills the men, she'll have to run. Sooner or later she'll have to kill again, or they'll catch her. She'll continue to hate them. Arrow doesn't want that.

After the cellist disappeared, Arrow went down to the street. She looked at the broken windows and the pile of flowers. She didn't think of anything. She just stood there. This was the cellist's last day. The music in the street was finished. Arrow put her rifle next to the cellist's bow and walked away.

Soon, the door will open. There will be four men, maybe more. As quickly as possible, they'll fire bullets into her. It won't take long.

She hears one of them step back. She knows that he's going to kick in the door. She closes her eyes. She remembers the notes that she heard only yesterday. The music feels very close.

Just before the door flies open, she speaks. Her voice is strong and quiet.

'My name is Alisa.'

ACTIVITIES

Chapter 1

Before you read

1 Find Sarajevo on a map of Europe. What do you know about its history, and about the siege of the city in the 1990s? Use the Internet to learn more.

2 Read the Introduction to the book. Why did Steven Galloway write this story?

3 Look at the Word List at the back of the book, and then make sentences with these pairs of words.
   a bow – cello
   b bullet – rifle
   c container – handle
   d explode – shell
   e fire (v) – sniper

While you read

4 Answer these questions
   a Who decides not to buy bread?

   ....

   What happens to the bread line?

   ....

   b Who shoots a soldier?

   ....

   Where is she hiding?

   ....

   c Who checks his water containers?

   ....

   Where is he going?

   ....

   d Who walks along 'Sniper Street'?

   ....

   Where is he going?

   ....

After you read

5 Discuss these questions.

    a Why does Arrow think that she is different from the snipers on the hills?

    b Why did she change her name?

    c How does Kenan feel when he leaves the flat?

    d How can he carry six containers?

    e Why is Dragan going to the bakery?

    f Why does he live with his sister?

6 Work with another student. Act out this phone call.

    Student A: You live in Sarajevo at the time of this story. Tell Student B what the city is like.

    Student B: You lived in Sarajevo in the 1980s. You remember how Sarajevo was then. Ask questions about places in the city and about the way of life now.

Chapter 2

Before you read

7 Discuss these questions. What do you think?

    a Will the cellist play the Adagio again?

    b What problems will Kenan have on his way to the brewery?

    c Will the men on the hills find Arrow?

While you read

8 Number these sentences in the right order, 1–9.

    a The bird is pulled into the doorway and the man kills it.   .....

    b Kenan goes past a large square.   ..1..

    c The old man walks away with his bag of dead birds.   .....

    d A bird moves past him.   .....

    e The man pulls the stick with the rope on it.   .....

    f He sees an old man sitting in a doorway.   .....

    g It disappears into the doorway of a building.   .....

    h He ties bread to the rope, then throws it into the square.   .....

    i The bird eats the bread.   .....

9 Discuss the purposes of:
   a   the food centre
   b   the tunnel under the airport
   How helpful do they seem to be to ordinary people?

10 Nermin says to Arrow, 'Don't worry, your hands will stay clean.' What do you think he means?

Chapter 3

Before you read

11 What can Arrow do to protect the cellist? How can she keep him alive? What problems will she have? Discuss these questions with another student.

While you read

12 Are these sentences right (✓) or wrong (✗)?
   a   Dragan sees Emina and wants to talk to her.   .....
   b   Emina is taking some medicine to her mother.   .....
   c   Dragan is almost shot on the crossing.   .....
   d   Arrow doesn't want to protect the cellist.   .....
   e   She sees a shadow in a fourth floor room.   .....
   f   Two girls put flowers at the feet of the cellist.   .....
   g   Kenan walks past the National Library.   .....
   h   A woman crosses the bridge with him.   .....
   i   There are not many people at the brewery.   .....

After you read

13 Why do you think the sniper didn't shoot the cellist?

14 Kenan thinks that everyone is testing the snipers at the crossings. What do you think he means by this?

Chapter 4

Before you read

15 What do you think happens next? Choose the best answer(s).
   a   Emina is shot on the crossing.
   b   The brewery is shelled.

    c   Ismet helps Kenan carry his water home.

    d   A sniper kills the cellist.

    e   Arrow kills the sniper.

    f   The sniper kills Arrow.

While you read

  16 Who is speaking?

    a   'I don't understand how you're not afraid.' ....

    b   'Maybe he's playing for himself'. ....

    c   'I'm afraid that this war isn't a war'. ....

    d   'Maybe I'll get back in time to hear the cellist.' ....

    e   'I can't go yet, I'm not ready.' ....

  17 Who or what do the words in *italics* describe?

    a   *He's* watching *her*. ....
    ....

    b   It's clear that *he's* listening to the music. ....

    c   *He* knows that *it*'s going to fall near him. ....
    ....

    d   *They*'re heavy, but with three on each side *he* can do it. ....
    ....

After you read

  18 Discuss why:

    a   Emina tells Dragan about the cellist, and it makes him uncomfortable.

    b   the sniper doesn't shoot the cellist.

    c   Kenan throws himself onto the ground and cries.

  19 Work with another student. Have this conversation.

    Student A: You are Arrow. You are reporting to Nermin after you shot the sniper. Tell him about it.

    Student B: You are Nermin. Ask Arrow some questions. You want to know exactly what happened.

Chapter 5

Before you read

20 Look at the title of Chapter 5. Who do you think has to disappear?

21 What do you think will happen next to these people?

   a Emina

   b the cellist

   c Arrow

   d Nermin

While you read

22 Put these words in the right sentences. Use each word only once.

   protection   medicine   commander   explosion

   decisions   bullet   guns   tunnel

   a The .... has hit the top of Emina's arm.

   b Dragan takes the .... out of Emina's coat pocket.

   c Dragan imagines going through the ....

   d Nermin tells Arrow that he can't give her .... now.

   e There is an .... inside Nermin's office building.

   f Three men with .... take Arrow away.

   g Karaman is Arrow's new ....

   h He will make the .... for her now.

After you read

23 Discuss which words best describe Nermin, Karaman or neither.

frightening	understanding	cold
friendly	dangerous	hard
amusing	sad	good-looking
pleasant	nervous	kind
strong		

24 At the end of the chapter, Karaman explains the war to Arrow. Do you think he is right? Discuss this with other students.

25 Life is going to be very different now for Arrow. What do you think she will do next?

Chapter 6

Before you read

26 Who do you think is in the most danger now: Dragan, Kenan, Arrow or the cellist? Why?

27 If the cellist is shot now, what do you think will happen?

While you read

28 Complete these sentences with 1–5 below.

a	Cars come through the tunnel	.....
b	They take out things	.....
c	The same businessmen buy and sell	.....
d	Ismet's army pay only buys	.....
e	The rice was given to Sarajevo free	.....

1) a small bag of rice.

2) the city's water.

3) with things to sell.

4) by foreign countries.

5) that Sarajevans can't use now.

After you read

29 Arrow is now in great danger. Did she do the right thing? What do you think?

30 Work with another student. Imagine that Dragan visits Emina in hospital.

Student A: You are Emina. Tell Dragan about the journey to hospital. Ask him what happened at the crossing.

Student B: You are Dragan. Explain why you moved the body from the street.

Chapter 7

Before you read

31 Why do you think this chapter is called *The Last Day*? Is there more than one possible reason? What do you think is going to happen?

While you read

32 Complete the sentences.

    a Kenan worries about .... clothes and ....
for the winter.

    b He doesn't want to go .... but he has to get
....

    c He has listened to the .... every day at .... o'clock.

    d Dragan feels more .... when he doesn't ....
across the road.

    e He takes the .... to the address on the paper
before he goes to the ....

    f Arrow is woken by the heavy .... of ....
outside her flat.

    g She watched the cellist until his .... day, and then
she left her .... with his bow and the flowers.

After you read

33 Discuss these questions with other students.

    a Why does the cellist drop his bow onto the pile of flowers?

    b Why does Arrow put her rifle next to the cellist's bow?

    c Why does Arrow decide not to shoot the men at her door?

Writing

34 You work for a newspaper. You are in Sarajevo to report on the
war. Write about one of the crossings in the city. Describe the
people that you see. What happens while you are there?

35 Write a conversation between Dragan's son, Davor, and an
Italian friend. Davor is now twenty years old and he is in Italy
with his mother. He doesn't want to go home to Sarajevo after
the war. His friend is surprised.

36 Write a description of Kenan's flat. How do you think it looks
inside? What can he and his family see from their windows?
What do they own – and what have they sold?

37 Make a list of the things that people in Sarajevo did not have
during the siege. Put them in order of importance to you.

38 You are an old friend of Arrow's. You were at university together. Write a letter to another friend. Tell him/her that you have heard about Arrow's death. Write about how you remember her. (You should use her real name.)

39 Imagine that the siege of Sarajevo has just ended. Dragan and Kenan meet for the first time. They are in the street where the cellist played. Write their conversation.

40 Imagine that after the war Ismet becomes a taxi driver again. One day he drives Dragan's wife, Raza, to the city centre. Write their conversation.

41 What do you think happened to the cellist in this story after the war? Did he stay in Sarajevo? Did he play the cello again? Write about his life.

42 Which person in the book do you like best? Why?

43 Imagine that it is now fifteen years after the story ends. What has changed in Sarajevo? Have the people in this story changed? How? Write a short chapter.

WORD LIST

army (n) the soldiers of a country

bakery (n) a place where bread and cakes are made

bow (n) the special stick used with a cello. You play the cello by pulling the bow across it.

brewery (n) a place where beer is made

bullet (n) a small piece of metal that is shot from a gun

cello (n) a large wooden box with rounded sides, used to play music. You hold it between your knees and pull a bow across it. A **cellist** is a person who plays the cello.

commander (n) an officer in the army

container (n) something like a bag or a box that you keep things in

control (n/v) the ability to make all the important decisions about a place or people

explode (v) to make a sudden, loud noise, usually as something is destroyed. This is an **explosion**.

fire (v) to shoot a gun. When you shoot, the sound of **gunfire** is heard.

handle (n) the part of something that you hold it by

rifle (n) a long gun. You hold it against your shoulder when you shoot.

rope (n) something long, strong and thick that you tie things with

ruin (n) the part of a destroyed building that is still standing

shell (n/v) something that is shot from a large gun. It can destroy buildings when it hits them.

siege (n) a time when enemy soldiers are all around a city. People can't leave the city, and food and other things can't go in. The city is **under siege**.

sniper (n) someone who shoots at people from a hiding-place

tunnel (n) a path under the ground for cars or trains

tuxedo (n) a special black suit or jacket worn by men for important parties and for some weddings. Professional male musicians sometimes wear tuxedos when they play to people.